Igor Stravinsky

# PETRUSHKA
## and
# THE RITE OF SPRING
### for
# PIANO FOUR HANDS
### or
# TWO PIANOS

DOVER PUBLICATIONS, INC.

NEW YORK

# PUBLISHER'S NOTE

Though both pieces in this volume were originally specified for piano four hands ("piano à quatre mains"), there are passages in both that are impossible to play as written on a single piano. This is the reason for the ambiguity in the volume's title.

Published in Canada by General Publishing Company, Ltd., 30 Lesmill Road, Don Mills, Toronto, Ontario.
Published in the United Kingdom by Constable and Company, Ltd.

This Dover edition, first published in 1990, is an unabridged republication in one volume of the two following works: (1) *Pétrouchka: scènes burlesques en 4 tableaux d'Igor Strawinsky et Alexandre Benois; réduction pour piano à quatre mains par l'auteur*, originally published by Edition Russe de Musique (Russischer Musikverlag), Berlin, Moscow, St. Petersburg, 1913; and (2) *Le sacre du printemps: tableaux de la Russie païenne en deux parties d'Igor Strawinsky et Nicolas Roerich; réduction pour piano à quatre mains par l'auteur*, Edition Russe de Musique, 1914. In the present edition, a new English translation of the introductory texts replaces the Russian and French versions. The French section headings and stage directions have been replaced by new English translations on the music pages, but the French (corrected!) appears in the new table of contents.

Manufactured in the United States of America
Dover Publications, Inc., 31 East 2nd Street, Mineola, N.Y. 11501

**Library of Congress Cataloging-in-Publication Data**

Stravinsky, Igor, 1882–1971.
   [Petrushka; arr.]
   Petrushka ; and, The rite of spring.

   Ballets, originally for orchestra; arr. by the composer.
   Reprint (1st work). Originally published: Pétrouchka. Berlin : Edition russe de musique, 1913. Pl. no.: R.M.V. 150.
   Reprint (2nd work). Originally published: Le sacre du printemps. Berlin : Edition russe de musique, 1914. Pl. no.: R.M.V. 196.
   1. Ballets—Piano scores (4 hands) I. Stravinsky, Igor, 1882–1971. Vesna sviashchennaia; arr. 1990. II. Title: Petrushka. III. Title: Rite of spring.
M1523.S92P44    1990           89-756056
ISBN 0-486-26342-8

# CONTENTS

*The original score had headings and stage directions in Russian and French. In the present edition, the French is replaced by a new English translation on the score pages, but the French wording is preserved in this table of contents.

# THE RITE OF SPRING*          83

*The original Russian headings appear on the corresponding music pages. The English renderings of them given here reflect Stravinsky's own mature preferences. A few renderings that differ, but have been hallowed by usage, are supplied in square brackets. The French versions of the titles, added here in italics, are taken from the original score.

As a curiosity that may possibly be of some use to researchers, the following represents a novel (perhaps foolhardy) attempt to translate the original Russian headings into recognizable English, but also literally (as if each component Russian word really had a meaning of its own): "THE KISS BESTOWED UPON THE EARTH," "Introduction," "Springtime Soothsayings: Dance of the Fashionable Girls [or Women]," "The Simulated Abduction," "Vernal Round Dances," "The Game of the Two Towns [*or* Walled Settlements]," "The Procession of the Eldest-Wisest [Man]," "The Kiss Bestowed Upon the Earth (the Eldest-Wisest)," "The Figured Dance in Honor of the Earth [*or* The Acquisition of the Earth Through Dancing]," "THE GREAT SACRIFICE," "Mysterious Games of the Girls: Movement in Circles," "The Honoring of the Chosen One [female]," "The Appeal to the Forefathers," "The Ritual Performance of the Elders as the Forefathers of Mankind," "The Great Sacred Dance (the Chosen One)."

# PETRUSHKA

Burlesque Scenes in Four Tableaux
by Igor Stravinsky and Alexandre Benois

*Александръ Бенуа*

TO ALEXANDRE BENOIS

# PETRUSHKA

## Premiere Performance at the Théâtre du Châtelet
### (Paris, 13 June 1911)

## Under the Management of
## SERGE DE DIAGHILEV

Artistic director: Alexandre Benois. Choreographic director: Michel Fokine.

———————————

| Characters | Cast |
|---|---|
| The Ballerina [La Ballerine] . . . . . . . . . . . . . . . | Tamara Karsavina |
| Petrushka [Pétrouchka] . . . . . . . . . . . . . . . . . . . | Vaslav Nijinsky |
| The Moor [Le Maure] . . . . . . . . . . . . . . . . . . . | Aleksandr Orlov |
| The Old Magician [Le vieux Charlatan] . . . . . . . | Enrico Cecchetti |

The Wet-Nurses [Les Nourrices (Nounous)]: Baranovich I, Baranovich II, A. Vasilieva, M. Vasilieva, Gachevska, Tchernycheva, Lastchilina, Sazonova, Biber.

The Coachmen [Les Cochers]: Lastchilin, Semënov, Petrov, V. Romanov, Orlik.

The Grooms [Les Palefreniers]: Rosaï, A. Molotsov.

The Reveling Merchant [Le Marchand fêtard]: Koussov.

The Gypsy Women [Les tziganes]: Schollar, Reisen.

The Street Dancers [Les danseuses de rue]: Bronislava Nijinska, Vassilievska.

First Organ-Grinder [Premier joueur d'orgue]: Sergheiev.

Second Organ-Grinder [Second joueur d'orgue]: Kobelev.

The "Died" (master of ceremonies) [Le "Died" (compère de la foire)]: Romanov.

The Peepshow Exhibitor [Le montreur de vues d'optique]: Ognev.

Mummers and maskers [Masques et travestis]: Larionova, Kandina; Leontiev, Kremniev, Ulanov, S. Molotsov, Dmitriev, Gouduin, Kotchetovsky, Masslov, Gerassimov, Christapson, Larosov.

Shopkeepers (male and female) [marchands, marchandes], Officers [officiers], Soldiers [soldats], Noblemen [seigneurs], Ladies [dames], Children [enfants], Housemaids [bonnes], Cossacks [cosaques], Policemen [agents de la police], A Bear-Tamer [un montreur d'ours], etc.

### Conductor: Pierre Monteux
Scenes and dances choreographed and directed by Michel Fokine

Sets and costumes designed by Alexandre Benois

Sets built by Boris Anisfeld

Costumes sewn by Caffi and Vorobiev

# GENERAL NOTE

The action takes place in St. Petersburg, in Admiralty Square, around 1830. In addition to the ordinary curtain, there is a special curtain for the "burlesque scenes." This curtain represents the Magician, grandiosely portrayed, enthroned on the clouds. The ordinary curtain rises when the music begins and falls at the end of the show. The special curtain rises a bit later and falls between the tableaux.*

I. A sunny winter day. At the left, a large booth with a balcony for the "Died" (master of ceremonies). Beneath it, a table with a gigantic samovar. In the middle of the set, the Magician's little theater; at right, stalls selling sweets and a peepshow. At the rear can be seen merry-go-rounds, swings, and slides. A crowd of strollers onstage, including common people, gentlemen and ladies, groups of drunkards arm in arm; children surrounding the peepshow; women crowding around the stalls.

II. Petrushka's cell. Its cardboard walls are painted black, with stars and a half-moon. Figures of devils on a gold background decorate the leaves of the folding doors that lead into the Ballerina's room. On one of the cell's walls, the portrait of the scowling Magician (a bit below and to the side is where Petrushka punches a hole in his fit of despair).

III. The Moor's cell. Wallpaper with a pattern of green palms and fantastic fruits on a red background. The Moor, in a costume of great splendor, is lying on a very low sofa and playing with a coconut. To the right, the door that leads to the Ballerina's cell.

IV. The same set as in the 1st tableau. Toward the end, an effect of late evening. At the entrance of the mummers, Bengal lights are lit in the wings. At the moment of Petrushka's death it begins to snow and the darkness deepens.

---

*There are precise indications in the score for raising and lowering the two curtains.

# "PETRUSHKA"
## (Burlesque Scenes in 4 Tableaux)

In the midst of the Shrovetide festivities, an old Magician of oriental appearance exhibits before an astonished crowd the animated puppets Petrushka, the Ballerina, and the Moor, who perform a wild dance.

The Magician's magic has endowed them with all the human feelings and passions. Petrushka has been given more than the others. Therefore he suffers more than the Ballerina and the Moor. He resents bitterly the cruelty of the Magician, his bondage, his exclusion from ordinary life, his ugliness, and his ridiculous appearance. He seeks comfort in the love of the Ballerina, and is on the point of believing in his success. But the lovely one shuns him, feeling only terror at his bizarre behavior.

The Moor's life is completely different. He is brutish and wicked, but his splendid appearance fascinates the Ballerina, who tries to seduce him using all her charms and finally succeeds. Just at the moment of the love scene, Petrushka appears, enraged with jealousy, but the Moor quickly throws him out the door.

The Shrovetide fair is at its height. A reveling merchant accompanied by gypsy singers throws handfuls of bank notes to the crowd. Coachmen dance with wet-nurses, a bear-tamer appears with his beast, and finally a band of mummers sweeps everyone up in a diabolical melee. All at once cries are heard from the Magician's little theater. The rivalry between the Moor and Petrushka finally takes a tragic turn. The animated puppets dash from the theater, and the Moor knocks Petrushka down with a blow of his saber. The wretched Petrushka dies in the snow, surrounded by the holiday crowd. The Magician, whom a policeman has gone to fetch, hastens to reassure everyone, and in his hands Petrushka becomes a puppet again. He invites the crowd to verify that the head is wooden and the body is filled with bran. The crowd disperses. The Magician, now alone, catches sight, to his great terror, of Petrushka's ghost above the little theater, menacing him and making mocking gestures at all whom the Magician has fooled.

# КАРТИНА ПЕРВАЯ.
## НАРОДНЫЯ ГУЛЯНІЯ НА МАСЛЕНОЙ.

# FIRST TABLEAU
## The Shrovetide Fair.

СПЕЦІАЛЬНЫЙ ЗАНАВѢСЪ.
Special Curtain.

ПРОХОДИТЪ, ПРИПЛЯСЫВАЯ НЕБОЛЬШАЯ ТОЛПА ПОДПИВШИХЪ ГУЛЯКЪ
A Group of Drunken Revelers Passes, Dancing.

БАЛАГАННЫЙ ДѢДЪ СЪ ВЫСОТЫ СБОЕГО БАЛАГАНА ПОТѢШАЕТЪ ТОЛПУ.
The Master of Ceremonies Entertains the Crowd from His Booth Above.

ШАРМАНЩИКЪ НАЧИНАЕТЪ ИГРАТЬ.
The Organ-Grinder Begins to Play.

УЛИЧНАЯ ТАНЦОВЩИЦА, ТАНЦУЕТЪ, ОТБИВАЯ ТАКТЪ ТРЕУГОЛЬНИКОМЪ.
The Dancer Dances, Beating Time on the Triangle.

(*) ШАРМАНЩИКЪ, ПРОДОЛЖАЯ ОДНОЙ РУКОЙ ВЕРТѢТЬ ШАРМАНКУ, ДРУГОЮ ИГРАЕТЪ НА КОРНЕТѢ-А-ПИСТОНѢ.
The Organ-Grinder, Continuing to Turn the Crank with One Hand, Plays the Cornet with the Other.

НА ДРУГОМЪ КОНЦѢ СЦЕНЫ ИГРАЕТЪ ЯЩИКЪ СЪ МУЗЫКОЙ,
ВОКРУГЪ КОТОРАГО ТАНЦУЕТЪ ДРУГАЯ УЛИЧНАЯ ТАНЦОВЩИЦА.

At the Other End of the Stage a Music Box Plays, Another
[Woman] Dancer Dancing Around It.

[come sopra]

ПЕРВАЯ ТАНЦОВЩИЦА СНОВА БЬЕТЪ ВЪ ТРЕУГОЛЬНИКЪ. The First Dancer Plays the Triangle Again.

Triangl.

ШАРМАНКА И ЯЩИКЪ СЪ МУЗЫКОЙ ПЕРЕСТАЮТЪ ИГРАТЬ; БАЛАГАННЫЙ ДѢДЪ СНОВА ПРИВЛЕКАЕТЪ ВНИМА-
The Organ and the Music Box Stop Playing; the Master of Ceremonies Resumes His Pitch.

String. ♪.♩ = 46

String. ♪.♩ = 46

(★) ШАРМАНЩИКЪ СНОВА ИГРАЕТЪ НА КОРНЕТ - А - ПИСТОНѢ.
The Organ-Grinder Begins to Play the Cornet Again.

ВОЗВРАЩАЕТСЯ ВЕСЕЛАЯ КОМПАНIЯ ГУЛЯКЪ.
The Merry Group Returns.

Timp.

Long drum and side drum onstage.

ИЗЪ ТЕАТРИКА ПОЯВЛЯЕТСЯ СТАРЫЙ ФОКУСНИКЪ.
At the Front of [i.e., from inside] the Little Theater Appears the Old Magician.

## ФОКУСЪ.

## THE MAGIC TRICK.

Lento. ♩=50

Lento. ♩=50

ФОКУСНИКЪ ИГРАЕТЪ НА ФЛЕЙТѢ.
The Magician Plays the Flute.

(lunga)

ЗАНАВѢСЪ ТЕАТРИКА РАЗДВИГАЕТСЯ; ТОЛПА
The Curtain of the Little Theater Opens and the

ВИДИТЪ ТРИ КУКЛЫ: ПЕТРУШКУ, АРАПА И БАЛЕРИНУ.
Crowd Sees Three Puppets: Petrushka (Guignol), a Moor, and a Ballerina.

ФОКУСНИКЪ ОЖИВЛЯЕТЪ ИХЪ ПРИКОСНОВЕНІЕМЪ СВОЕЙ ФЛЕЙТЫ.
The Magician Brings Them to Life by Touching Them Lightly with His Flute.

ПЕТРУШКА, АРАПЪ И БАЛЕРИНА ДРУЖНО ПУСКАЮТСЯ ВЪ ПЛЯСЪ КЪ ВЕЛИКОМУ УДИВЛЕНІЮ ВСѢХЪ.

Petrushka, the Moor, and the Ballerina Suddenly Begin to Dance, to the Great Astonishment of the Crowd.

ТЕМНОТА ЗАНАВѢСЪ.
Darkness. Curtain.

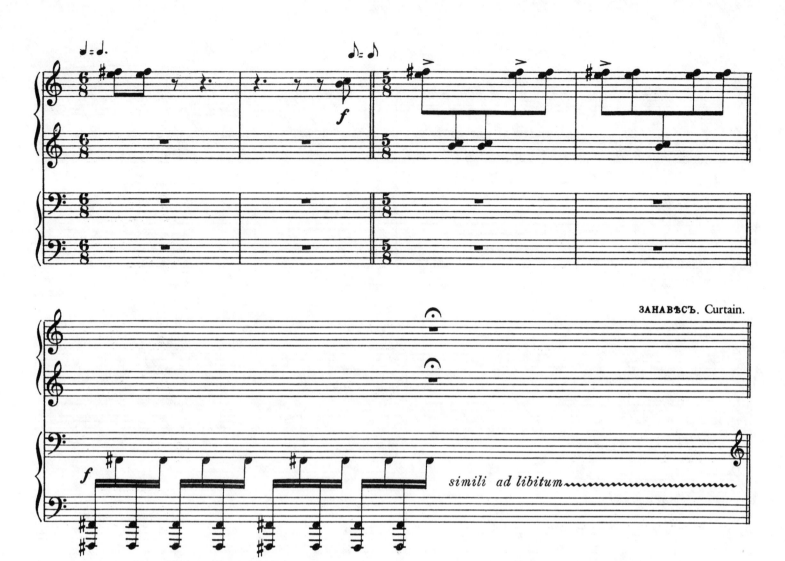

# КАРТИНА ВТОРАЯ.
### У ПЕТРУШКИ.

ЗАНАВѢСЪ. Curtain.

# SECOND TABLEAU
### Petrushka's Room.

ПРИ ПОДНЯТІИ ЗАНАВѢСА ДВЕРЬ ВЪ КОМНАТКѢ У ПЕТРУШКИ ВНЕЗАПНО ОТВОРЯЕТСЯ; ЧЬЯ - ТО НОГА ГРУБО ЕГО ВЫТАЛКИВАЕТЪ; ПЕТРУШКА ВАЛИТСЯ. ДВЕРЬ ЗА НИМЪ ЗАТВОРЯЕТСЯ.

As the Curtain Rises, the Door to Petrushka's Room Opens Suddenly; a Foot Kicks Him Onstage; Petrushka Falls and the Door Closes Again Behind Him.

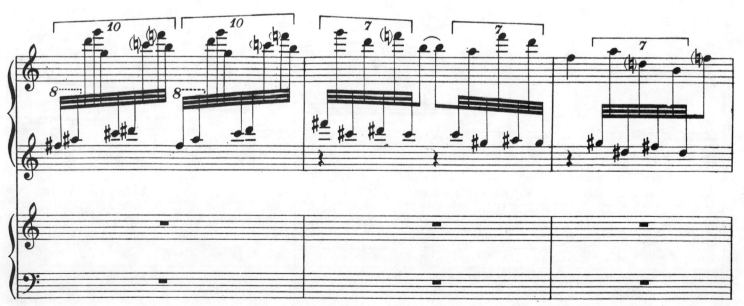

ВХОДИТЪ БАЛЕРИНА.
The Ballerina Enters.

Meno mosso. ♩= 72

ОТЧАЯНИЕ ПЕТРУШКИ.
Petrushka's Despair.

ТЕМНОТА. Darkness.
ЗАНАВѢСЪ. Curtain.

# КАРТИНА ТРЕТЬЯ.
## У АРАПА.

# THIRD TABLEAU
## The Moor's Room.

ЗАНАВѢСЪ. Curtain.

# ТАНЕЦЪ БАЛЕРИНЫ.
## (СЪ КОРНЕТЪ-А-ПИСТОНОМЪ ВЪ РУКѢ.)

# DANCE OF THE BALLERINA
### (Cornet in Hand).

# ВАЛЬСЪ.
## (БАЛЕРИНА И АРАПЪ.)

# WALTZ
## (The Ballerina and the Moor).

АРАПЪ И БАЛЕРИНА ПРИСЛУШИВАЮТСЯ.
The Moor and the Ballerina Prick Up Their Ears.

ПОЯВЛЕНІЕ ПЕТРУШКИ.
Appearance of Petrushka.

СCOPA АРАПА СЪ ПЕТРУШКОЙ. БАЛЕРИНА ПАДАЕТЪ ВЪ ОБМОРОКЪ.
The Fight Between the Moor and Petrushka. The Ballerina Faints.

**Agitato.** ♩.= 100

АРАПЪ ВЫТАЛКИВАЕТЪ ПЕТРУШКУ. ТЕМНОТА. ЗАНАВѢСЪ.
The Moor Throws Petrushka Out. Darkness. Curtain.

# КАРТИНА ЧЕТВЕРТАЯ

## НАРОДНЫЯ ГУЛЯНІЯ НА МАСЛЕНОЙ
### (ПОДЪ ВЕЧЕРЪ)

# FOURTH TABLEAU
The Shrovetide Fair (Toward Evening).

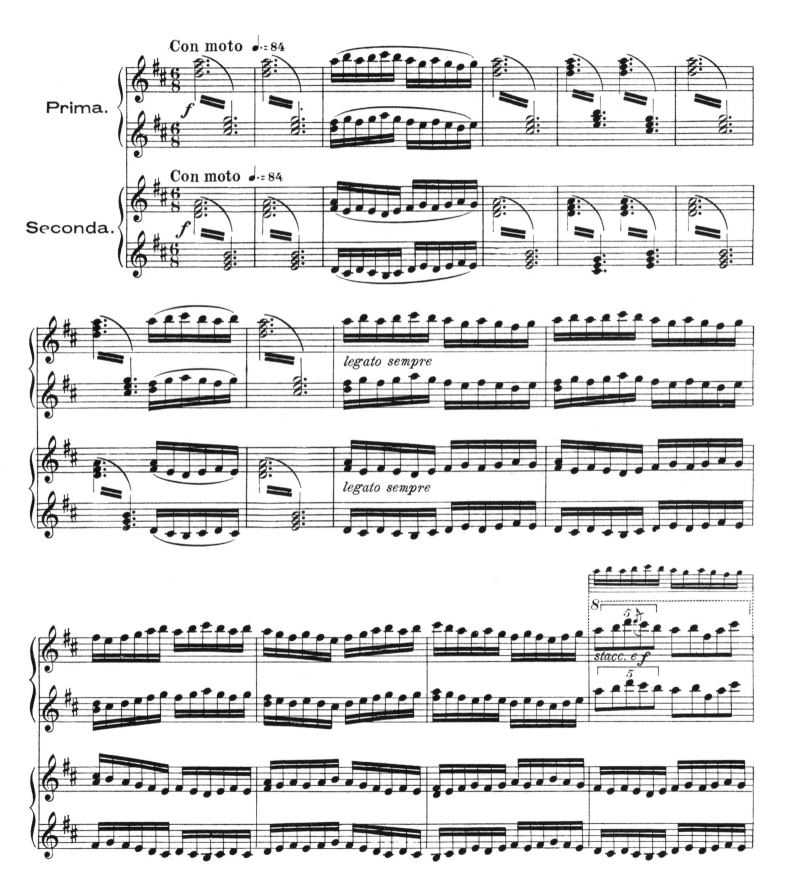

ЗАНАВѢСЪ. Curtain.

ff legato sempre

ff

# ТАНЕЦЪ КОРМИЛИЦЪ.

## THE WET-NURSES' DANCE.

ВХОДИТЪ МУЖИКЪ СЪ МЕДВѢДЕМЪ. ВСѢ КИДАЮТСЯ ВЪ СТОРОНУ.
A Peasant Enters with a Bear. Everyone Scatters.

МУЖИКЪ ИГРАЕТЪ НА ДУДКѢ—МЕДВѢДЬ ХОДИТЪ НА ЗАДНИХЪ ЛАПАХЪ.

The Peasant Plays the Pipe. The Bear Walks on His Hind Feet.

МУЖИКЪ СЪ МЕДВѢДЕМЪ УДАЛЯЮТСЯ.

The Peasant and the Bear Leave.

ВВАЛИВАЕТЪ УХАРЬ-КУПЕЦЪ СЪ ДВУМЯ ЦЫГАНКАМИ. ВЪ РАЗГУЛЬНОМЪ ВЕСЕЛІИ СВОЕМЪ ОНЪ БРОСАЕТЪ ТОЛПѢ КИПЫ АССИГ-
A Reveling Merchant and Two Gypsy Women Enter. He Irresponsibly Amuses Himself by Throwing Bank Notes to the Crowd. НАЦІЙ.

ЦЫГАНКИ ТАНЦУЮТЪ. КУПЕЦЪ ИГРАЕТЪ НА ГАРМОНИКѢ.
The Gypsy Women Dance. The Merchant Plays the Accordion.

КУПЕЦЪ И ЦЫГАНКИ УДАЛЯЮТСЯ.
The Merchant and the Gypsies Leave.

## ТАНЕЦЪ КУЧЕРОВЪ И КОНЮХОВЪ.

## DANCE OF THE COACHMEN AND THE GROOMS.

КОРМИЛИЦЫ ТАНЦУЮТЪ ВМѢСТѢ СЪ КУЧЕРАМИ И КОНЮХАМИ.
The Wet-Nurses Dance with the Coachmen and the Grooms.

РЯЖЕННЫЕ.  THE MUMMERS.

БАЛАГУРСТВО РЯЖЕННЫХЪ (КОЗЫ СО СВИНЬЕЙ)
Buffoonery of the Mummers (Goat and Pig).

МАСКИ И РЯЖЕННЫЕ ТАНЦУЮТЪ.
The Mummers and the Maskers Dance.

ОСТАЛЬНЫЕ ПРИСОЕДИНЯ‐
The Rest of the Crowd Joins

-ЮТСЯ КЪ ПЛЯСКѢ РЯЖЕНЫХЪ.
in the Mummers' Dance.

ПЛЯСКА ПРЕКРАЩАЕТСЯ. ПЕТРУШКА ВЫБѢГАЕТЪ ИЗЪ ТЕАТРИКА, ПРЕСЛѢДУЕМЫЙ АРАПОМЪ,
The Dances Break Off. Petrushka Dashes from the Little Theater, Pursued by the Moor, Whom the

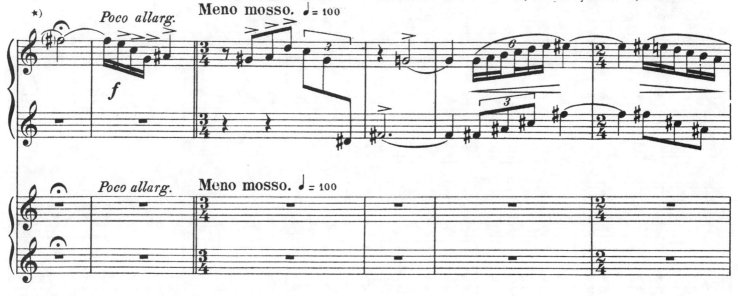

КОТОРАГО БАЛЕРИНА СТАРАЕТСЯ УДЕРЖАТЬ.
Ballerina Tries to Restrain.

*) ТОЛПА ПРОДОЛЖАЕТЪ ТАНЦОВАТЬ, НЕ ОБРАЩАЯ НИКАКОГО ВНИМАНІЯ НА КРИКИ, ДОНОСЯЩІЕСЯ ИЗЪ МАЛЕНЬКАГО ТЕАТРИКА.
The Crowd Continues to Dance Without Taking Notice of the Cries Coming from the Little Theater.

ВЗБѢШЕННЫЙ АРАПЪ ЕГО НАСТИГАЕТЪ И
The Furious Moor Seizes Him and Strikes Him

УДАРЯЕТЪ СВОЕЙ САБЛЕЙ.
with His Saber.

ПЕТРУШКА ПАДАЕТЪ СЪ РАЗ-
БИТЫМЪ ЧЕРЕПОМЪ.
Petrushka Falls, His Head
Broken.

Tambourine.

ТОЛПА ОКРУЖАЕТЪ ПЕТРУШКУ.
A Crowd Forms Around Petrushka.

ОНЪ ЖАЛОБНО УМИРАЕТЪ.
He Dies, Still Moaning.

ПОСЫЛАЮТЪ БУДОЧНИКА ЗА ФОКУСНИКОМЪ.
A Policeman Is Sent to Look for the Magician.

ПРИХОДИТЪ ФОКУСНИКЪ.
The Magician Arrives.

ОНЪ ПОДЫМАЕТЪ ТРУПЪ ПЕТРУШКИ И ТРЯСЕТЪ ЕГО.
He Picks up Petrushka's Corpse, Shaking It.

НАРОДЪ РАСХОДИТСЯ.
The Crowd Disperses.

ФОКУСНИКЪ ОСТАЕТСЯ ОДИНЪ НА СЦЕНѢ.  ОНЪ ТАЩИТЪ ТРУПЪ ПЕТРУШКИ ВЪ ТЕАТРИКЪ.
The Magician Remains Alone on the Stage. He Drags Petrushka's Corpse toward the Little Theater.

НАДЪ ТЕАТРИКОМЪ ПОЯВЛЯЕТСЯ ПРИВИДѢНІЕ ПЕТРУШКИ, ГРОЗЯЩЕЕ И ПОКАЗЫВАЮЩЕЕ ДЛИННЫЙ НОСЪ ФОКУСНИКУ. ФОКУСНИКЪ
Above the Little Theater Appears the Ghost of Petrushka, Menacing, Thumbing His Nose at the Magician. The Terrified Magician Lets the

ВЪ УЖАСѢ ВЫПУСКАЕТЪ ИЗЪ РУКЪ КУКЛУ-ПЕТРУШКУ И, БОЯЗЛИВО ОЗИРАЯСЬ, ПОСПѢШНО УХОДИТЪ.
Puppet-Petrushka Drop from His Hands and Exits Quickly, Casting Frightened Glances over His Shoulder.

ЗАНАВѢСЪ.
Curtain.

ROME MAI 1911.

# THE RITE OF SPRING

(literally, Holy Spring)

Scenes of Pagan Rus' [Russia] in Two Parts
by Igor Stravinsky and Nikolai Roerich

_Николаю Константиновичу_

_Рериху_

TO NIKOLAI KONSTANTINOVICH ROERICH

# THE RITE OF SPRING

Premiere Performance at the Théâtre des Champs-Elysées
(Paris, May 1913)

Under the Management of
SERGE DE DIAGHILEV

Directed by
IGOR STRAVINSKY and VASLAV NIJINSKY

Choreography by
VASLAV NIJINSKY

Sets and Costumes by
NIKOLAI ROERICH

# ЧАСТЬ ПЕРВАЯ.
## ПОЦѢЛУЙ ЗЕМЛИ.

### Вступленіе.

# FIRST PART
## A KISS OF THE EARTH

### Introduction

Занавѣсъ. День.
Curtain. Day.

Появленіе
Entrance of the Young Girls.

щеголихъ.

ВЕШНІЕ ХОРОВОДЫ.

SPRING ROUNDS

*Remove finger from key.

ПОЦѢЛУЙ ЗЕМЛИ.
[Старѣйшій-Мудрѣйшій.]

# THE KISS OF THE EARTH
### (The Oldest and Wisest One)

ВЫПЛЯСЫВАНІЕ ЗЕМЛИ.

# THE DANCING OUT OF THE EARTH

Занавѣсъ.
Curtain.

# ЧАСТЬ ВТОРАЯ.
## ВЕЛИКАЯ ЖЕРТВА.

### Вступленіе.

# SECOND PART
## THE EXALTED SACRIFICE

### Introduction

Занавѣсъ. — Curtain.  Ночь. — Night.

# ТАЙНЫ ИГРЫ ДѢВУШЕКЪ
# ХОЖДЕНІЕ ПО КРУГАМЪ.

# MYSTIC CIRCLE OF
# THE YOUNG GIRLS

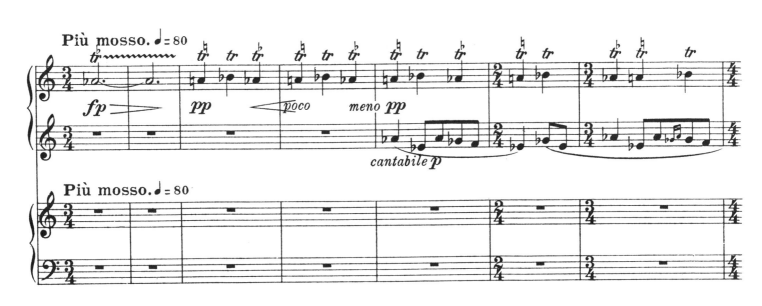

Дѣвушки останавливаются. Указаніемъ судьбы одна изъ нихъ обречена на великую жертву. Избранница стоитъ
The Dance Is Interrupted. One of the Girls Is Designated by Fate as the Sacrificial Victim.   The Chosen One Remains Immobile

неподвижно до великой священной пляски.
Until the Sacrificial Dance.

## ВЕЛИЧАНІЕ ИЗБРАННОЙ.

## THE NAMING AND HONORING
## OF THE CHOSEN ONE

**136**   *THE RITE OF SPRING*

ВЗЫВАНІЕ КЪ ПРАОТЦАМЪ.

# ВЕЛИКАЯ СВЯЩЕННАЯ ПЛЯСКА.
## [Избранница.]

# SACRIFICIAL DANCE
## (The Chosen One)